Someone was tapping at his window. It was his friend Rosie. “Donald!” she cried. “It’s an emergency!”

Donald's home was behind the stage at Walnut Elementary School.
"Yuk!" said Donald. "There's a river in my house!"

'hat's what I came to tell you," said Rosie. "It's not
ıst here, it's the whole school! Jump on! We have to
ɔ something – and quick!"

Donald and Rosie sailed down the rushing water to the bottom of the stairs, barely hanging on. Then suddenly ...

Rosie toppled into the swirling waters. "Help!" she cried. "I'm drowning!"

"Hold on," said Donald. "I'll save you."

Donald reached Rosie and bravely pulled her up ontc
something floating by.
"It's a good thing this boat came along."

“It’s not a boat,” said Rosie. “It’s Noah’s Ark! The children have been learning about The Flood in school.”

“Let’s go in and explore!” said Donald.

Donald and Rosie crept inside the ark as the water carried it along.
"Look, there's two of everything," said Donald.
"Just like us," said Rosie.

Suddenly there was a BANG! on the roof.
"What was that?" cried Rosie.
"Sounds like something big has landed on the boat,"
said Donald. "I'll go up and look."

“It’s a bird!” Donald shouted to Rosie. “But he’s not hurt. He’s just lost his breath.”
Donald stroked the bird’s head as the ark sailed into the school kitchen.

“Look! Here’s the problem!” Donald explained.
He pulled and tugged until the water finally shut off.

"Whew," said Donald.
And they all went inside the ark to rest from their watery adventure.

Later, the ark came to a stop. “Is it dry enough to go outside now?” asked Rosie.
“Perhaps our friend will fly out and take a look around for us,” said Donald.

As Donald and Rosie watched the bird fly away, they heard some familiar voices.

It was the children coming back to their classroom.
"Oh, no!" one boy shouted.
"Let's work together to clean up this mess," said the teacher.

As the children picked up the chairs, one friendly boy discovered the ark ... and Donald and Rosie.

“Look,” said the boy. “There really are two of everything in Noah’s Ark – even two sweet little mice!”

When the teacher saw Donald and Rosie, she SCREAMED!
The children all giggled and laughed.

That's when Donald and Rosie decided it was time to go.

Donald and Rosie went out into the Spring sunshine t
dry off and saw the most amazing rainbow!
“Why do we have rainbows?” wondered Donald.
“We’ll have to find out,” Rosie answered.